The Secret of the Sacred Temple:
CAMBODIA

Join Secret Agent Jack Stalwart

on his other adventures:

The Escape of the Deadly Dinosaur: **USA**

The Mystery of the Mona Lisa: **FRANCE**

The Search for the Sunken Treasure: **AUSTRALIA**

The Secret of the Sacred Temple:
CAMBODIA

Elizabeth Singer Hunt

Illustrated by Brian Williamson

RED FOX

THE SECRET OF THE SACRED TEMPLE: CAMBODIA
A RED FOX BOOK 978 1 862 30296 9

First published in Great Britain by Chubby Cheeks Publications Limited
Published in this edition by Red Fox,
an imprint of Random House Children's Books

Chubby Cheeks edition published 2005
This edition published 2006

The Random House Group Limited makes every effort to ensure that the papers used in its
books are made from trees that have been legally sourced from well-managed and credibly
certified forests. Our paper procurement policy can be found at:
www.randomhouse.co.uk/paper.htm

Set in Meta, Trixie, American Typewriter, Luggagetag, Gill Sans Condensed and Serpentine.

Red Fox Books are published by Random House Children's Books,
61–63 Uxbridge Road, London W5 5SA.
A Random House Group Company

www.**kids**at**random**house.co.uk

Addresses for companies within The Random House Group Limited can be found at:
www.randomhouse.co.uk/offices.htm

THE RANDOM HOUSE GROUP Limited Reg. No. 954009

A CIP catalogue record for this book is available from the British Library.

Printed and bound in Great Britain by Cox & Wyman Ltd, Reading, Berkshire

For the people of Southeast Asia,
my 'home away from home'

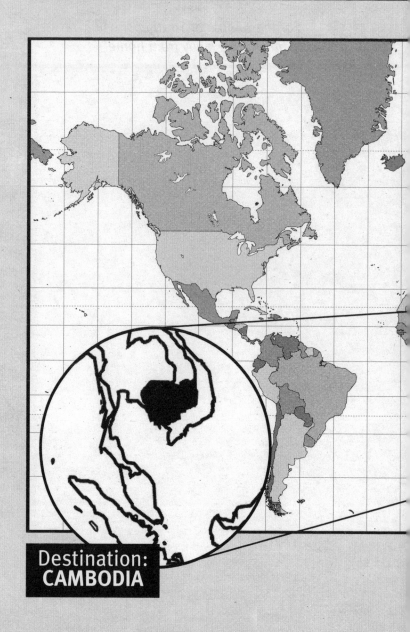

Destination:
CAMBODIA

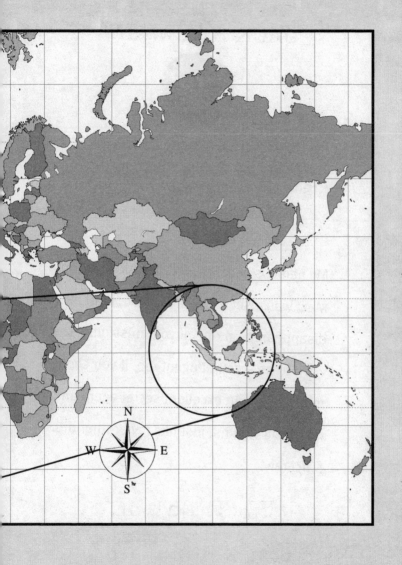

JACK STALWART

Jack Stalwart applied to be a secret agent for the Global Protection Force four months ago.

My name is Jack Stalwart. My older brother, Max, was a secret agent for you, until he disappeared on one of your missions. Now I want to be a secret agent too. If you choose me, I will be an excellent secret agent and get rid of evil villains, just like my brother did. Sincerely,

Jack Stalwart

GLOBAL PROTECTION FORCE INTERNAL MEMO:
HIGHLY CONFIDENTIAL

Jack Stalwart was sworn in as a Global Protection Force secret agent four months ago. Since that time, he has completed all of his missions successfully and has stopped no less than twelve evil villains. Because of this he has been assigned the code name 'COURAGE'.

Jack has yet to uncover the whereabouts of his brother, Max, who is still working for this organization at a secret location. Do not give Secret Agent Jack Stalwart this information. He is never to know about his brother.

Gerald Barter

Gerald Barter
Director, Global Protection Force

THINGS YOU'LL FIND IN EVERY BOOK

Watch Phone: The only gadget Jack wears all the time, even when he's not on official business. His Watch Phone is the central gadget that makes most others work. There are lots of important features, most importantly the 'C' button, which reveals the code of the day – necessary to unlock Jack's Secret Agent Book Bag. There are buttons on both sides, one of which ejects his life-saving Melting Ink Pen. Beyond these functions, it also works as a phone and, of course, gives Jack the time of day.

Global Protection Force (GPF): The GPF is the organization Jack works for. It's a worldwide force of young secret agents whose aim is to protect the world's people, places and possessions. No one knows exactly where its main offices are located (all correspondence and gadgets for repair are sent to a special PO Box, and training is held at various locations around the world), but Jack thinks it's somewhere cold, like the Arctic Circle.

Whizzy: Jack's magical miniature globe. Almost every night at precisely 7:30 p.m., the GPF uses Whizzy to send Jack the identity of the country that he must travel to. Whizzy can't talk, but he can cough up messages. Jack's parents don't know Whizzy is anything more than a normal globe.

The Magic Map: The magical map hanging on Jack's bedroom wall. Unlike most maps, the GPF's map is made of a mysterious wood. Once Jack inserts the country piece from Whizzy, the map swallows Jack whole and sends him away on his missions. When he returns, he arrives precisely one minute after he left.

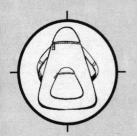

Secret Agent Book Bag: The Book Bag that Jack wears on every adventure. Licensed only to GPF secret agents, it contains top-secret gadgets necessary to foil bad guys and escape certain death. To activate the bag before each mission, Jack must punch in a secret code given to him by his Watch Phone. Once he's away, all he has to do is place his finger on the zip, which identifies him as the owner of the bag and immediately opens.

THE STALWART FAMILY

Jack's dad, John

He moved the family to England when Jack was two, in order to take a job with an aerospace company. As far as Jack knows, his dad designs and manufactures aeroplane parts. Jack's dad thinks he is an ordinary boy and that his other son, Max, attends a school in Switzerland. Jack's dad is American and his mum is British, which makes Jack a bit of both.

Jack's mum, Corinne

One of the greatest mums as far as Jack is concerned. When she and her husband received a letter from a posh school in Switzerland inviting Max to attend, they were overjoyed. Since Max left six months ago, they have received numerous notes in Max's handwriting telling them he's OK. Little do they know it's all a lie and that it's the GPF sending those letters.

Jack's older brother, Max

Two years ago, at the age of nine, Max joined the GPF. Max used to tell Jack about his adventures and show him how to work his secret-agent gadgets. When the family received a letter inviting Max to attend a school in Europe, Jack figured it was to do with the GPF. Max told him he was right, but that he couldn't tell Jack anything about why he was going away.

Nine-year-old Jack Stalwart

Four months ago, Jack received an anonymous note saying: 'Your brother is in danger. Only you can save him.' As soon as he could, Jack applied to be a secret agent too. Since that time, he's battled some of the world's most dangerous villains, and hopes some day in his travels to find and rescue his brother, Max.

DESTINATION:
Cambodia

The temple of Angkor Wat was built by a king called Suryavarman II (pronounced *Surrey-ya-varmin*) between 1113 and 1150

●

Cambodia is located in Southeast Asia

●

The word Angkor means 'city'

●

The capital city of Cambodia is Phnom Penh (pronounced *Pe-nom Pen*)

●

The word Wat means 'temple'

●

Fourteen million people live in Cambodia

●

The official language of Cambodia is Khmer (pronounced *Ka-mare*)

●

The largest river in Southeast Asia, the Mekong, flows through Cambodia

●

The main religion in Cambodia is Buddhism

The Great Travel Guide

SECRET AGENT PHRASEBOOK FOR CAMBODIA

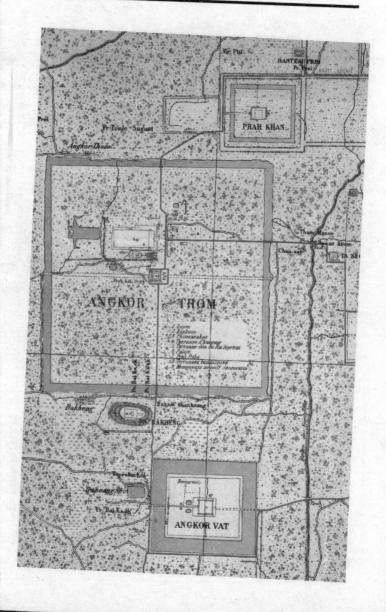

Cambodia

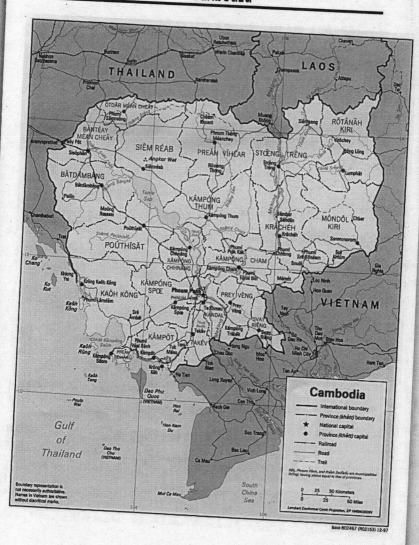

SECRET AGENT GADGET INSTRUCTION MANUAL

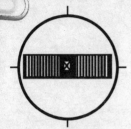

Transponder: Ideal for tracking a friend or an evil villain. Just place this small, sticky plastic piece on someone (or something) and activate the 'T' button on your Watch Phone. Instantly, the location of the Transponder will appear.

TRACKING DISTANCE: 50 miles

Mine Alert: Imbedded into every standard-issue secret-agent shoe. Just flick the 'alert' switch on the outside of your shoe and wait for a green light to come out of the tip. As soon as you start to move, the Mine Alert lasers sweep the territory ahead, sending vibrations through your shoe if you're about to step on a bomb.

Electrolyte Dust:

Whenever you've been knocked senseless by your opponent or feel dehydrated, just peel open the orange pack and sprinkle the dust on your tongue. It will instantly revive you and restore important salts to your body, making you feel refreshed.

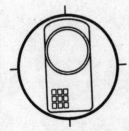

Body-Count Tracker:

An excellent hand-held device for mapping out a location before you've even entered it. The Body-Count Tracker will show you where the walls, doors, windows and ceilings are located in every room and whether there are any people inside. It can also tell you whether they are alive or dead, a useful tool for any secret agent entering the unknown.

Chapter 1:
The Annoying One

'And then you'll never guess what happened,' gushed Lily, Jack's eleven-year-old cousin. She was visiting Jack's family from Devon, where Jack's Aunt Emma, Lily's mum, lived. 'My friend Luke stood in front of the class to read his essay and didn't even know that his shirt-tail was stuck in the zip of his trousers! Isn't that embarrassing?'

The whole family – Jack, his dad, his mum and Lily – were sitting around the dinner table finishing a delicious fish-and-chip supper. If the story had

1

been told by anyone else, Jack would have found it funny. But because it was told by his annoying cousin, he just rolled his eyes and looked at his mum.

'That's a nice story, Lily,' said Jack's mum to Lily. 'Did anything exciting happen to you today?' she asked, turning her attention to Jack.

Just as Jack was about to tell his family about how he had scored a corker of a goal in today's football match, he spied the clock hanging on the wall above his mother's head. It read 7:28 p.m. He looked back at his mum and smiled before he leaped from his chair and headed for the kitchen door.

'Lots of stuff, Mum,' said Jack, 'but it'll have to wait until tomorrow. I've got maths homework to do!' He left the kitchen and quickly climbed the stairs to his bedroom.

Jack's dad, who had up until now listened silently to the conversation at the table, said proudly, 'It's wonderful that Jack has taken such an interest in maths.'

As Jack began to open his bedroom door, he could hear his cousin talking again downstairs. 'Guess what happened to my friend Frieda McCauley today?' she squealed excitedly to her aunt and uncle.

'Someone stole a hairbrush out of her bag!'

Poor Mum and Dad, Jack thought, shaking his head. Glad I have some maths homework. He smiled to himself as he opened the door and stepped into his top-secret bedroom.

Chapter 2:
The Secret

Jack entered the room, hung his 'KEEP OUT' sign on the doorknob and closed the door behind him. There was always the possibility that a family member would walk in and discover something Jack didn't want them to see – like Whizzy telling him about his next mission, or Jack surveying his latest hi-tech gadgets.

Jack was a secret agent for the Global Protection Force. The Global Protection Force, or GPF, sent Jack around the globe in order to protect the world's most precious people, places and things.

'*Protect that which cannot protect itself*' was the motto of the Global Protection Force. The organization was started in 1947 by a man named Ronald Barter who decided he'd had enough of crooks trying to destroy things that mattered in the world. Things like beautiful pieces of art, endangered animals, famous buildings, or even famous people who were trying to do something positive. When he died in 1962 (in mysterious circumstances), his son Gerald took over and made the GPF one of the leading worldwide forces against crime.

Jack joined the GPF after his older brother, Max, disappeared. Although no one else in his family knew that Max was a secret agent for the GPF, Jack did. That was because Max had told him.

Max used to show Jack his secret-agent gadgets and explain how they worked as he told him stories about using each one on his missions. Jack looked forward to those times with Max so he could hear all about the adventures. Although lots of brothers their age didn't get on, Jack and Max got on well. They were more like best friends.

Then Max was sent by the GPF to a supposed school in Switzerland.

When Jack received the anonymous note telling him his brother was in danger, he quickly signed up to join the GPF and dedicated his life to finding Max. As soon as he was on the 'inside', he asked the GPF about Max's whereabouts, but the GPF wouldn't tell Jack a thing. They denied any involvement in Max's disappearance and immediately sealed Max's files.

Even so, Jack always hoped that one of his missions would lead to some information about Max. Who knows? thought Jack that evening, maybe this mission will be the one.

Chapter 3:
The Foreign Land

Suddenly, there was a buzzing sound
from the side of Jack's bed. Whizzy, Jack's
magical miniature globe, was spinning
hard to try to get Jack's
attention and to build
up enough speed to
hurl the jigsaw piece
inside him out onto
the floor.

'Ahem!' Whizzy
coughed. A jigsaw
piece flew out of
his mouth so fast

that it hit the wall opposite and bounced back onto the floor near Jack's desk.

Jack walked over and picked up the piece. Looking at it, he had no idea what country it could be. There was nothing distinctive about it. No long bits. No short bits. Just a rounded country that didn't look like anywhere in particular.

Jack carried the piece over to his wall where there was an amazing map of the world, with every single country carved into it. One morning, not long after he was sworn in at the GPF, Jack woke up and found the map there. Now, how was he going to explain *this* to his parents, he thought. In the end, he just shrugged and said that it was a prize from one of his teachers.

He picked up the piece and started to move it over the map. He was looking for that 'perfect fit', where the jigsaw piece slotted neatly into a country on the wall.

As Jack's hand stroked the map, his eyes scanned the continents. Not America, not Africa, not Europe. What about Asia? He glanced at India (which was too big) and started going over Burma and Thailand. Just past Thailand, Jack looked at the wall and noticed something. The shape of the jigsaw piece and the shape of the country to the southeast of Thailand matched. He pushed the piece onto the wall and it snapped in. The name 'CAMBODIA' flashed on the wall once and then disappeared.

'Cambodia?' said Jack, completely surprised. As far as he knew, it was now a peaceful country without much need for the likes of the GPF.

Just as Jack was trying to remember everything he'd learned about the country in his GPF training, a pink light inside Cambodia started to glow. He didn't have much time.

Jack hurried across his room and reached under his bed. He grabbed his Secret Agent Book Bag then pushed the 'C' button on his Watch Phone. The word T-E-M-P-L-E appeared on the mini-screen. He punched the letters into the lock on

his Book Bag and it immediately opened.

Jack quickly checked that all the essential gadgets were inside. The old standbys – the Magic Key Maker, the Expand-A-Rope and the Net Tosser – were there, along with new tools like the Depth Barometer, the Body-Count Tracker and the Voice-Recognition Passport.

He locked his Book Bag, hurried over to the wall and stood before it just as the pink light grew to fill his entire room. When he knew the time was right, he yelled, 'Off to Cambodia!' The pink light flickered and burst, swallowing Jack into his Magic Map.

Chapter 4:
The Drop Off

The next thing Jack knew he was falling head first out of the sky towards the ground below. He was travelling so fast that he could feel the skin on his face being pushed backwards towards his ears.

Directly below him he could see a massive, ancient temple surrounded by water and hidden in the jungle. The temple looked beautiful, like something out of an *Indiana Jones* or *Tomb Raider* movie. But this wasn't the time to admire beautiful works of architecture. Not when

he was about to be splattered all over it.

Just need to reach a bit further, he told himself as he strained to find the small cord attached to his Secret Agent Book Bag. He knew that if he pulled the string, it would release a hidden parachute from his bag, which would carry him gently to the ground.

SNAP! Jack pulled the cord. Nothing happened. He lifted his hand in front of his face, his eyes widening when he saw the small bit of the string he was holding. Panic filled his body as he realized the parachute was broken.

Jack was now falling fast. Near the monument, he could see a gathering of people. They had noticed him hurtling towards the ground without a parachute and were crowding together, anxious to see what would happen.

Quickly, he tucked his knees close to

his chest and reached for his left shoe. He twisted open the heel of the shoe and grabbed a small disc from inside. This was The Dome, a small, round disc with a highly elastic material inside, normally used by secret agents as an expandable bag. Since he didn't have a parachute, he had no choice but to try The Dome instead. He somersaulted in the air so that his feet were facing the ground and lifted the disc high above his head using both hands. As he continued to fall, the elastic material began to expand like a balloon. It took all Jack's strength to hold onto it, but The Dome was acting just like a normal parachute, helping to slow down his descent.

He was only ten metres from the ground when, without warning, the elastic material inside The Dome burst. Jack dropped straight towards the ground.

Luckily for him, it wasn't the ground but the water near the monument that broke his fall.

SPLASH!

Jack landed feet first in the dirty, murky water. When his head came up again, he gasped for air. The crowd that had gathered started to shout and cheer.

19

It wasn't every day that someone fell out of the sky without a parachute and lived to tell the tale.

As Jack looked at the crowd, a girl of about his own age bent down.

'You must be Jack,' she said. 'Here, let me help you out,' she offered, extending her hand.

Jack paused for a second, confused as to how this young girl knew who he was. He noticed that she was wearing a

necklace with a medallion on it. On the medallion was an image of a man with four hands. Jack reached up towards the girl and put his hand in hers.

When she had pulled Jack out of the water and onto the walkway, she looked at him. 'My name is Kate,' she said. 'Nice of you to drop in,' she added. A smile spread across her face. 'I've been waiting for you.'

Chapter 5:
The Mission

'What? You're my contact?' he asked, wiping the water off his face. 'I don't understand. Normally,' he added, 'I'd be meeting with an adult.'

'Well, I'm sorry to disappoint you,' Kate said, wrinkling her mouth at Jack, 'but I am the one who called the GPF. My mum told me to call them if anything happened. And, well' – she paused, her voice breaking slightly – 'since it has, I thought I should call right away.'

'What do you mean?' he asked. 'What's happened?'

In the split second it took before she answered the question, Jack took a proper look at Kate. Nice green eyes. Nice smile. Nice curly brown hair. Plus, she wasn't loud like his cousin Lily. Instead, she had a soft-sounding voice. Loud girls were always annoying as far as Jack was concerned.

'My mum's been kidnapped,' Kate said. The statement snapped Jack out of his private thoughts.

'Kidnapped?' he asked. 'When? Where? Why?'

'Yesterday,' said Kate. 'I came home from school and the house was a mess. I waited for hours for my mum to come home from work at the temple but she never did.'

'What do you mean "the temple"?' asked Jack. 'Which one was she working on?'

'You know, the ancient temple of Angkor

23

Wat,' she said. 'You nearly fell on it before landing in the water.'

Jack looked at the enormous temple behind him. It had five pointed towers, the middle one of which was the tallest. The temple was huge. It was awe-inspiring.

'The temple of Angkor Wat was one of

many temples built in the ancient city of Angkor,' Kate explained. 'The city was built by the Khmer people of Cambodia about a thousand years ago. At that time, the Khmers were very powerful and ruled much of Southeast Asia.' Kate paused and then carried on. 'In order to pray to their gods and bury their kings, they built a series of temples, one of which was Angkor Wat. Then, in the fifteenth century, the Thai people invaded from across the border in Thailand, and the Khmers fled, leaving the temples behind.'

'Who looked after the temples then?' asked Jack.

'Over the years,' answered Kate, 'the jungles grew over them and hid them completely. They weren't discovered again until the nineteenth century. Since that time,' she added, 'archaeologists have been trying to protect them. The weather here is harsh and people try to steal artefacts from the temples, as they're worth a lot of money.'

'So why are you and your mum here?' asked Jack.

'My mum is one of the chief archaeologists watching over the temple of Angkor Wat,' said Kate proudly. 'We moved here a few months ago.'

'But why would someone want to kidnap your mum?' asked Jack. 'It sounds as if she was trying to help.'

'I don't know,' said Kate, shrugging her shoulders and looking down at the walkway. 'That's why I contacted the GPF. I don't think I can find my mum without your help.'

Jack thought about what Kate was saying. Although this seemed like the straightforward kidnapping of an important person, he couldn't help but

feel that there was something more
sinister going on. He needed more facts.

'Where was your mother last seen?'
asked Jack.

'At home,' said Kate. 'I'll take you
there.'

'Great,' said Jack, following Kate as she
set off along the walkway.

Chapter 6:
The Clue

When they arrived at Kate's house, escaping the humid weather outside, Jack was surprised at the terrible state it was in. The house was an absolute mess. Tables had been turned upside down. Pictures had been ripped from the walls. Curtains had been shredded to bits. Pretty much everything that had been standing on its own legs was now overturned on the cold stone floor.

Quickly, Jack walked around the house, making sure it was safe and that there was no one else inside. He came back to

Kate, who was standing in the lounge.

Jack took a few minutes to think. He wondered whether the mess was because of a struggle between Kate's mum and her captors, or if it was because someone was looking for something they thought Kate's mum had.

'When I came home from school,' explained Kate, 'the house was like this and my mum was missing. Now do you see why I called the GPF?'

'Sure do,' said Jack, still amazed at the sight of Kate's house.

'What should we do?' asked Kate. 'How are we going to find my mum? The jungle around the temples is huge – she could be anywhere by now.'

Jack inspected the room more carefully. If there had been a struggle between Kate's mum and her captors, the house wouldn't have looked this bad. No, thought Jack. This was definitely the result of someone looking for something. But what?

'Did your mum keep anything valuable in the house, like one of those artefacts from the temples?' asked Jack.

'No,' said Kate. 'Mum didn't take anything from the temples.'

Jack's eyes were roaming around the room, looking for clues that might lead them in the right direction. He lifted up the upside-down tables and chairs and looked at the darker patches on the walls where the pictures had hung. As far as Jack could tell, there weren't any false walls or secret compartments in the house where Kate's mum could have hidden something.

Jack bent down to check under the sofa. As he was looking, he spied a small rectangular box. He grabbed it and brought it out into the light of the room. He took a closer look.

'That's my mum's voice recorder,' said Kate.

'A voice recorder?' said Jack curiously.

'You know,' explained Kate, 'a tape recorder. My mum took it wherever she went

so that she could record her observations
and then play them back later in the day.'

Jack looked inside the small cassette
window. The tape seemed to be at the
end of Side A. Jack rewound it and
pushed the 'play' button. He turned up
the volume and listened.

A frightened female voice began to
speak: 'To whoever finds this tape, this is
Rachel Newington, Chief Archaeologist
and protector of the temple of Angkor

Wat. At any moment, the forces of darkness will descend, searching for the map of the central well. The map must be sent away before they acquire it. Find my daughter and—'

CRASH! There was the sound of breaking glass.

'Oh my God,' the woman whispered into the recorder, 'they're here!'

SLAM! A door hit the wall as it was flung open. Then there was the sound of the voice recorder being dropped and kicked across the floor.

'Hello, Rachel,' said a man's voice, which grew louder as he walked further into the room. 'So nice to see you again.'

'Get out of my house!' she shouted. 'Get out of Cambodia!'

'Come now, Rachel,' said the man. 'There's no need to be difficult. I'm sure you know why we're here. Just hand it over and all will be well.'

'I'll never give you the map!' she screamed. 'You'll have to kill me first!'

The man laughed nastily. 'That part's negotiable, my dear,' he said. 'Let's make this easy. Hand over the map.'

'Never!' she screamed.

'Chai!' shouted the man. There was the sound of someone else walking into the room. 'Why don't you escort Rachel to the Temple of the Trees and we'll see whether we can't force the location of the map out of her?'

There were muffled sounds of Kate's mum being dragged away. Then the door closed.

CRASH! It sounded as though furniture was being thrown around.

SCREECH! Chairs were slid across the floor. Someone was still there.

'Where is it? Where is it, you dreadful woman?' the man demanded furiously.

'I'll find it, Rachel,' he cursed, 'whatever it takes!'

There was the sound of the man leaving the room and slamming the door behind him, then silence.

Chapter 7:
The Surprise

Jack turned off the tape recorder and looked at Kate. Tears were welling up in her eyes.

'Don't worry, Kate,' he said, trying to make her feel better. 'I'll find your mum. I promise.'

Kate sniffed the tears away. 'I know,' she said. 'I trust you. My mum said that if you were anything like your brother you'd be a terrific secret agent.'

Jack stood there, stunned into temporary silence.

'What do you mean, my brother?' he

said, almost too shocked to register what she had actually said. 'How do you know my brother?' he asked, his voice starting to quiver.

'Well, I don't know him personally,' Kate said, 'but my mum met him when she was working in Egypt. There were some problems on her project and she had to call the GPF. Your brother was the agent assigned to the case.'

'Egypt?' asked Jack. He had no idea his brother had been assigned to a project in Egypt. 'What else do you know?' he went on frantically. 'What do you mean there were problems? What kind of project was she working on? You have to tell me everything!'

'But I don't know any more,' said Kate. 'That's all I know. My mum said she'd heard that you'd become a secret agent too and that I should call you if anything happened. She trusted your brother, so I guess she decided to trust you too.'

Jack felt as if he was going to faint. He couldn't believe that he was sitting in the middle of this girl's house in the Cambodian jungle, hearing about his brother, Max, who'd been missing for four months. He had to find Kate's mum – not just because that was his assignment, but also because she must be able to tell him more about Max's disappearance.

'Right,' said Jack, with a new sense of urgency. 'We need to find your mum. The man on the tape mentioned the "Temple of the Trees". Any idea which of the temples that could be?'

'Well,' said Kate, 'a lot of the temples have trees around them, but there's only one that has trees inside it. They're growing through the walls, in fact,' she added. 'And that's the Temple of Ta Phrom.'

Chapter 8:
The Jungle

'Let's get going,' said Jack, tightening the straps on his Book Bag.

'It's too far to walk,' said Kate, 'we'll have to take the bikes.'

Jack and Kate hurried outside and grabbed two bicycles off the rack in front of Kate's house. Before setting off, Jack grabbed Kate's arm and pulled her back.

'Wait,' he said, handing her a small piece of plastic. 'Put this in your shoe.'

'What is it?' she asked.

'It's a Transponder,' said Jack.

'You know, so I can find you in case

you get lost or something.'

'Yeah, right,' said Kate. 'Like I'm going to get lost. I live here, remember. I know this place like the back of my hand! If anyone's going to get lost, it's you!'

'Well, it would make me feel better if you had it,' said Jack. He knew that his Watch Phone had a tracking device linked to the Transponder, so if she did get lost, he'd be able to find her.

'OK. OK,' she said as she reluctantly placed the Transponder in her shoe.

Kate pushed off and pedalled ahead, guiding Jack down a narrow dirt path and onto a road that led deep into the jungle. The longer they rode, the more difficult it was to see. The sun was setting fast and the road they were cycling on was shrouded by tall, leafy trees. Squinting, Jack could just about see Kate pedalling ahead and a family of fruit bats swarming above her.

After about ten minutes, Kate began to slow down. She pulled over to the side of the road and pushed her bike into the trees. Jack did the same and stood next to Kate. They had already agreed to park

the bikes away from the temple and
approach on foot.

'How far is it from here?' he asked.

'About a minute's walk,' she said,
pointing between the trees.

Jack stepped into the forest but Kate
grabbed his hand, pulling him back.

'Wait!' she said. 'You need to be careful.
There are lots of landmines in the ground.
They were left here during a civil war
years ago and some haven't been
detonated yet. I'd hate for you to be

blown up before we find my mum,' she added, smiling. Jack couldn't tell if she was joking or not.

In case she wasn't, Jack bent down towards his shoes and activated the Mine Alert. Instantly, two long green lights shot out of the tips of his shoes and began moving from side to side, like windscreen wipers, scanning the ground.

'Cool,' she said, looking down at Jack's feet.

'Yeah,' said Jack, pleased that his gadget had impressed her. 'These will tell us if there are any landmines ahead. Stick close,' he added, 'and step in exactly the same spots as me.'

'You got it,' said Kate, standing close behind him. Then they both headed off into the jungle, carefully winding their way towards the Temple of the Trees.

Chapter 9:
The Temple of
the Trees

As the forest began to clear, Jack could see the Temple of Ta Phrom in the distance. It was an eerie site, the kind of haunted-looking place that people paid good money to try to recreate for Halloween at home.

It had enormous silvery trees growing inside and through its walls. Their large roots slithered over the stone like the tentacles of a giant octopus. The roots were slowly prying the temple apart, one piece at a time. Large white patches of lichen covered its walls, sucking whatever nutrients it could find in the stone. Jack thought he could hear the temple moaning. He gulped and looked out of the corner of his eye at Kate. He was more than just a little bit nervous but he tried not to show it.

Jack took a deep breath and approached the temple's entrance. He unzipped his Book Bag and took out his Body-Count Tracker – a hand-held device that could tell you how many people were inside a building before you even entered it. It could also tell you whether they were alive or dead: a green figure meant alive, a red one dead. Jack switched it on and focused it at the door of the temple so it could scan the area.

He stared at the screen. A floor plan of the temple appeared, showing him the exact layout. Jack moved the arrow

buttons up and down, trawling through the image. From what he could tell, there were three people inside. Two green figures were standing together in one room, while another green body was alone in a different area. If Kate's mum was the body by itself that meant she was still alive!

'That must be your mum,' said Jack, pointing to the single green figure.

He walked ahead, using the Body-Count Tracker as a map of the temple. They stepped into the main entrance area and through an open courtyard. Jack looked above him at the sky. Thankfully, the moon was almost full, providing them with just the right amount of light to navigate the temple walls. Above them, he could hear the call of bats.

Facing them was a large square building. Quietly, they walked round the corner and to its left. In the moonlight, Jack could see a wall of carved dancers. They looked as though they were being strangled by the trees, whose finer roots had woven themselves tightly around their necks. Hopefully it wasn't a sign of things to come.

Jack looked again at the Body-Count Tracker. Up to the left was another building. This was where the lone figure was located. The other two people were still on the opposite side of the temple. Quickly, Jack and Kate passed underneath a stone lintel and into the other building. Sitting on the floor, bound and gagged next to a small candle, was Kate's mum.

'Mum!' exclaimed Kate in a loud whisper as she raced over to her mother and hugged her. She quickly untied the gag that was around her mother's mouth.

'Kate!' said her mum, gasping for air. 'You need to leave right now! Your life will be in danger if they see you!'

'There's no way I'm leaving without you, Mum,' said Kate.

'There's no time!' said Kate's mum, her eyes pleading with her daughter. 'You have to go without me. You have the map of the central well!'

'What do you mean I have the map?' said Kate, looking at her mum in disbelief. 'You didn't give me any map!'

Kate's mum looked at her and then at the necklace around Kate's neck; the one with the image of the man with four hands. Kate looked down at the necklace too.

She lifted the medallion up and turned it over. On the back there was an inscription written in a language Kate had never seen before. She looked questioningly at her mum.

'When I became Chief Archaeologist of the temple,' her mother explained quickly, 'I was entrusted with this necklace. On the back of the medallion is an ancient inscription which tells the exact location of the central well within the Temple of Angkor Wat. Deep inside the central well is the sacred treasure of the god-king. No one knows what the treasure looks like. Not only is it priceless, it's a source of power to whoever possesses it.'

'But how could anyone read what's on the back?' asked Kate, staring at the funny writings on the medallion.

'Only a few people in the world know how to decipher that language,' answered

Kate's mum. 'And, unfortunately, the man
who is after it is one of them.'

'Yes, that's right,' said a male voice
from behind. Jack spun round as two men
walked into the room. Jack recognized the
voice of the man who was speaking. It
was the one from the voice recorder. His
companion was a Thai man dressed in
silk pantaloon trousers.

'You've saved me a lot of trouble,' the
man continued, grinning from ear to ear.
Jack was temporarily stunned by his smile –
the top four teeth in the man's mouth were

not made of enamel, but of pure gold.

'How stupid of you, Rachel,' he said, looking at Kate's mum, 'to give something so valuable to such a young girl.'

'Shut up!' Kate shouted at the man. 'You'll never get the map from me!' she said, clutching the necklace in her hands.

'You sound just like your mother,' he said, laughing. His gold teeth were shining in the candlelight. 'Has anyone ever told you that you look just like her?' He walked over to Kate and stroked her cheek.

'Don't you touch her!' said Jack as he lunged for the man.

But within an instant the man had tossed some powder at Jack which blinded him and instantly made him feel sick. His throat started to swell, making it hard for him to breathe. He coughed and collapsed on the floor, feeling as if he was about to pass out. As Jack slipped in

and out of consciousness, he could hear Kate's voice. It sounded as though it was very far away.

'Jack!' she screamed. 'Wake up!'

Then, with Kate's voice sounding even more distant, Jack fell into a deep sleep.

Chapter 10:
The Turning Point

When Jack woke up, it was daytime and he was by himself. There was no Kate and no Kate's mum. Luckily they hadn't taken his Book Bag. Reaching inside and grabbing a small orange packet, Jack opened a sachet of Electrolyte Dust and shook it onto his tongue. Instantly he began to feel better. He sat for a moment and tried to make sense of things while he looked at the light pouring through the temple windows.

He reached into his back pocket and pulled out Kate's mum's voice recorder.

He rewound it and pushed the play button again.

'. . . this is Rachel Newington, Chief Archaeologist and protector of the Temple of Angkor Wat. At any moment, the forces of darkness will descend, searching for the map of the central well. The map must be sent away before they acquire it. Find my daughter and—'

Now the message made sense. As far as Jack could tell, the man with the gold teeth had been looking for the map to the central well and thought that Kate's mum had it. That was, of course, until Jack and Kate showed up at the temple with Kate wearing it around her neck. Goodness only knew what the man was going to do to Kate now. Jack was starting to feel sick again. He'd really messed things up this time. He closed his eyes and wondered how on earth he was going to find Kate.

With his eyes closed, Jack became aware of a noise in the distance. The noise was growing louder by the second.

BLEEP! BLEEP! BLEEP! It was coming from Jack's Watch Phone. He looked down at the screen.

Of course! thought Jack. At last something was going right. The noise was Kate's Transponder, which he'd temporarily forgotten about.

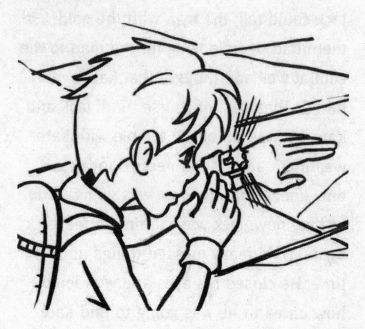

Quickly Jack punched the 'T' button on his Watch Phone. The words 'ANGKOR WAT, CAMBODIA' flashed across the screen and with it a tiny map of where it was located. The man with the gold teeth must have taken Kate and her mum along with him to the Temple of Angkor Wat to find the sacred treasure.

'I'm coming, Kate,' Jack said out loud as he picked himself up off the floor and raced out of the Temple of the Trees. He'd already been knocked out for hours. There was no time to waste.

Chapter 11:
The Path to
Angkor Wat

Jack found one of the bikes that he and
Kate had left in the jungle and pedalled it
as quickly as he could down the dirt road
towards Angkor Wat.

As he approached the temple, he began
to slow down. He surveyed the outside of
the massive monument. Angkor Wat was
surrounded by a moat filled with water,
the one that he had landed in yesterday.
Just inside the moat were high stone
walls that guarded the ancient temple
within. The only way in and out was on

the main walkway where he had first met Kate during his freefall arrival in Cambodia.

Since Angkor Wat was one of the first temples to be restored by the archaeologists, it had become something of a tourist attraction, with people walking in and out of its walls at all times of the day.

Unfortunately for Jack, that meant extra security precautions. Not only did he have to save Kate and her mum and protect the sacred treasure, but he also had to make sure that no tourists were harmed in the process.

Jack pedalled around the moat and approached the temple from the grand walkway. He hurried along, glancing at the people around him. Crowds were the perfect place for people to hide. He climbed the steps and passed through the first of two doors into the ancient temple grounds. Kate and her mum were nowhere to be seen.

Breathing heavily, he raced through the second door and into a bigger courtyard. He looked to the left, and then to the right. All he could see was tourists milling around. A group of people were taking photos of the strange carvings that lined the covered walkways along the perimeter.

He looked at his Watch Phone and

noted the location of Kate's Transponder. By the look of it, Jack was standing right next to her! But where was she?

It was faint, thought Jack, but he could have sworn he heard a girl scream. He looked at the tourists, who carried on taking photos. Another tour group passed by. Jack heard it again. No one in the temple besides Jack seemed to notice it. Maybe that powder had done something to his head and he was imagining things.

Jack looked ahead of him. In the middle of the courtyard was the fifth of the five towers, at the top of which was a small room. The only way up to the room was to climb the incredibly steep stairs, and each one was as high as Jack's legs were long.

'Jack!' It was the girl's voice again. It was Kate's and it was coming from inside the tower. He leaped up onto the first step. Using his hands and knees, he scrambled to the top of the steps and reached the entrance to the tower. Facing him was a sign that read: 'SANCTUARY CLOSED FOR REPAIRS'.

'Yeah, right,' said Jack as he hurried past the sign and into the tower.

He found himself standing in the middle of a small, square room with carvings of ancient people all around him.

'Help me!' screamed Kate. He could

hear her clearly now. But where was she? The echo in her voice made it sound as if she was at the bottom of a great cavern.

'Kate!' said Jack, scanning the room to try to find her. 'Where are you?'

'I'm down here!' she shouted. 'I'm in the central well!'

Jack ran to the middle of the room, stopping suddenly when he found himself teetering on the edge of a deep hole. He looked down into the hole, but couldn't see a thing. It was completely black. Kate must be scared to death down there.

'Hold on!' he shouted to her. 'I'll get you out of there!'

Jack yanked open his Secret Agent Book Bag and pulled out his Depth Barometer, which was a tiny round piece of plastic. Once Jack dropped it down the hole, it would feed back to his Watch Phone the exact depth of the well, which would tell

him how much rope he needed to rescue
Kate.

He tossed the Depth Barometer down
the hole and waited, looking at his Watch
Phone. A depth of twenty-three metres
flashed on the screen on his wrist. He

pulled his
Expand-
A-Rope
out of his
Book Bag

and programmed it to grow to twenty-
three metres in length. Then he tied one
end of the rope around his waist and
threw the other end down to Kate.

'I'm throwing you a rope!' he yelled. The
rope grew to precisely twenty-three metres
and fell straight into Kate's lap at the
bottom of the hole.

'Got it!' she yelled back.

'Right!' shouted Jack. 'Hold on!' He

braced himself and then programmed the rope to pull her gently upwards.

Jack peered down the entire time, waiting for Kate's face to appear in the darkness. When it did, he was overjoyed.

'Jack!' she screamed excitedly as she climbed out of the well and threw her arms around his neck. 'I knew you'd find me! But something terrible has happened! My mum,' she added frantically. 'They've taken her and the treasure too!'

'What do you mean?' asked Jack, untying the rope from his waist.

'After they drugged you,' explained Kate, 'the man ripped the medallion from my neck and read the back. The inscription told him to come here to the fifth tower. They kept us in a house until the morning and then brought us here, in case they needed my mum's help. When we got here, they realized that the well was too narrow for an adult, so they sent me down on a rope to the bottom.'

Kate took a deep breath and carried on. 'They told me to put whatever I found at the bottom of the well into a basket I'd been given and tie it to the end of the rope. Then I was supposed to yank on it to tell them that the treasure was ready. They were supposed to send the rope back down for me. But they didn't. And now they've got the treasure and my mum!'

'Did they say anything about where they were headed?' asked Jack.

'Not exactly,' answered Kate, 'but I think the man with the gold teeth was going back where he came from.'

From something Kate's mum had shouted at the man earlier, Jack knew that he didn't live in Cambodia. There was only one place he could be headed.

'The airport!' said Jack. 'We need to try

to stop them.'

Jack and Kate dashed out of the fifth tower and carefully descended the steep steps. They raced through the courtyard and the two doorways before reaching the grand causeway. At the end of the causeway there was a motorized scooter parked on the dirt road. Jack knew that if he borrowed it the GPF would return it to its rightful owner.

'Quick, hop on!' said Jack as he jumped onto the front of the scooter. Kate clambered on the back and put her arms around Jack's waist. Jack pulled the Magic Key Maker out of his Book Bag and inserted the long rubber tube into the ignition. Instantly, the rubber melted and then hardened again to form a perfect key for the ignition lock. Jack turned the key and the scooter fired up.

'Hold on tight!' he shouted to Kate as

the scooter lurched forward and sped off
down the road, leaving the Temple of
Angkor Wat in its dust.

Chapter 12:
The Airport

'This way!' shouted Kate, above the noise of the scooter's engine. She was pointing towards a large building next to a wide dirt track. 'That's the airport!' she yelled.

They turned right into the airport's car park and jumped off the scooter. They burst into the building and looked around. Hundreds of passengers, both local and foreign, were either waiting for their flights, or queuing to go through customs and immigration.

Jack and Kate frantically searched the room. If Kate's mum wasn't there, then they'd probably lost her for ever.

'Mum!' Kate shouted. She was looking towards the back of the building.

Jack followed her gaze. There, walking towards the back door, was Kate's mother. In front of her was the man with the gold teeth. Behind her was the Thai man, who seemed to be jabbing something into her back.

'Mum!' Kate shouted again. But the noise of the crowded airport drowned her out and Kate's mum didn't turn round.

'What are we going to do?' screamed Kate. 'They're going to take my mum away and I can't reach her! We can't get to the other side of the airport without a ticket!'

Jack thought for a moment. 'Wait here,' he said as he left Kate and moved quietly through the crowds to a place at the front of the immigration queue.

He rifled through his Book Bag and

pulled out his Voice-Recognition Passport and Trick Ticket. The Voice-Recognition Passport was one of the most useful things the GPF had ever invented. Whenever a secret agent said a name out loud, it transformed the name on the passport to the one the secret agent said. The Trick Ticket, which looked like a boarding card, worked in exactly the same way.

He glanced at the departures sign above and noticed a flight leaving in ten minutes to Thailand. It was flight 101. Jack lifted the Trick Ticket to his mouth and whispered, 'Flight 101. Thailand.' He then lifted the Voice-Recognition Passport to his lips and said, 'Somchai.' Jack knew Somchai was a Thai man's name.

'Next,' grunted the government official ahead. Jack stepped forward and presented his documentation.

FLIGHT NO.	DESTINATION
101	THAILAND
104	DELAYED

'Thank you,' said the official. 'Mr Somchai, is it?' he asked as he looked down at Jack's paperwork. He hesitated and Jack could tell the official was wondering how such a western-looking boy could have a common Thai name. But he couldn't very well ask. Instead, the official compared the name in the passport to the boarding card and paused.

'I hope you've had a nice stay in our country, Mr Somchai,' he said, handing Jack the passport and boarding card and nodding for him to proceed.

'Sure have,' said Jack, grabbing back his passport. Jack could see Kate's mum walking outside and onto the runway with the two men.

He dashed through the crowd and placed his Book Bag on the x-ray belt. He hustled through the arches of the security check and picked up his Book Bag, which was waiting for him on the other side. Thanks to the Anti-X-Ray feature on his Book Bag, the security guard checking his bag didn't see his gadgets. All they saw was a fake image of a pack of chewing gum, a couple of books and a handheld gaming device.

He raced out of the door. There, walking up the steps to a private plane, was Kate's mum, sandwiched between the Thai man, who had a gun in her back, and the man with the gold teeth, who was carrying a black box.

Now what was Jack going to do? This was the kind of situation the GPF always told its agents to try to avoid. It was almost certainly a no-win situation: a hostage situation involving a man with a gun and another with a priceless treasure. How was Jack going to rescue them both and get the bad guys?

Chapter 13:
The Switch

Jack crouched down and ran towards the
steps that led to the plane. He reached
into his pocket and pulled out a round
disc wrapped in black material. Holding
this in his hand, he stopped a few metres
from the steps of the plane.

'Hey, you!' he yelled up to the man with
the gold teeth. The Thai man plunged the
gun deeper into Kate's mum's back. Jack
could hear her wince.

The man with the gold teeth slowly
turned to look down at Jack from his
position at the top of the steps. His eyes

widened in anger and surprise when he saw Jack standing there.

'Yeah, you!' shouted Jack. 'Didn't you forget something?' He was holding the covered disc in his hand and waving it in the air.

'What do you mean?' asked the man, frowning at Jack.

'Seems like you forgot an important piece of the treasure!' said Jack, smiling as if he held an important secret.

'What is it?' he called over to Jack.

'Wouldn't you like to know?' said Jack, taunting the man. 'Kate gave it to me,' he added, 'when I rescued her from the fifth tower.'

The man looked at the airport building and spied Kate, who was frantically staring out through the window at the runway.

'That's impossible!' he said. 'I have it all!'

'Not so,' said Jack. 'Kate kept a piece back for herself. It's the most important piece, in fact. You can't do anything without it. It's the key to the treasure's power!'

The man furrowed his eyebrows and growled at Jack in anger.

'Of course,' said Jack, 'you can have it. But only after you release Kate's mum.'

He watched the man carefully. He could tell that he didn't know whether to trust

Jack or not. But fortunately the man was greedy, which is what Jack was counting on.

'All right, kid!' said the man, his gold teeth shining in the sun. 'You can have her, but only after I've looked at it. If it's a hoax,' he added, 'I'll kill both of you, instantly.'

'No way,' said Jack, feeling more and more confident. 'You're not going to get it until I get Kate's mum.'

The man paused for a second. 'Chai!' he yelled. With one push, the Thai man threw Kate's mum down the steps and she fell onto the runway. She lay on the ground for a few seconds before slowly picking herself up and looking at Jack.

'Thanks,' she mouthed to him as she rushed past and into the airport building to find Kate.

'Now hand it over!' The man scowled.

His patience was wearing thin.

The Thai man turned his attention to Jack. He lifted his gun and pointed it directly at him. Just then, the noise of the engines fired up. Jack didn't have much time. The plane was getting ready to leave.

'Hand it over!' the man yelled again.

Jack could tell he was getting angrier. But Jack still had one more thing to do: he had to get the treasure before the man took it on the plane and it was lost for ever. He looked carefully at the black box. It was tied shut with rope.

'OK,' said Jack, 'but you'll have to catch it!' He tossed the object high in the air, above the man's head.

'No!' screamed the man, dropping the black box in order to catch it with both hands. The disc slipped through his fingers and fell onto the steps of the

plane. Both the man with the gold teeth
and the Thai man were too busy fumbling
for the object to notice that Jack had
come up alongside them.

Jack reached into his Book Bag and
grabbed The Hook – an expandable hook

that allows you to grab things from a distance. Quietly, Jack slipped it through the railings and caught the rope on the black box. He pulled the box through the railings and snatched it away. The treasure was now in Jack's hands.

The man with the gold teeth hurried down the stairs, picked up the object and lifted it towards the sun. 'At last, we have the power!' he proclaimed to his henchman, who was now standing by his side. Neither realized that Jack had already snatched the box containing the treasure.

'I wouldn't say that,' said Jack as he reached into his Book Bag and pulled out the Net Tosser. The Net Tosser was a ring that when thrown opens up and casts a net. Jack flung it high over the two men. It burst open and fell on top of them, trapping them inside. The Thai man fired his gun at Jack, but the Net Tosser had a built-in 'anti-bullet' feature, which prevented any bullets from escaping to the outside. Instead, the bullet pinged around inside the net, with the men cowering for their lives.

The man with the gold teeth shouted from underneath the net. 'You'll never be able to activate the power of the treasure without this!' He lifted the object up towards Jack and unfolded the black material around it. The man looked at it with utter confusion.

'Green Day?' he said, reading the name on the disc. 'What is this, some kind of joke?'

'Not at all,' said Jack. 'They're a great band, in fact.

You'll have lots of time to listen to them when you're in prison.'

Jack used his Watch Phone to call the local authorities who, in addition to the security guards at the airport, descended on the men within minutes. They lifted the Net Tosser and took the Thai man's gun. Then both of them were cuffed on the spot.

'I'll get you for this!' the man screamed at Jack. 'This isn't the last you've seen of me, young man!'

The Thai man spat at Jack and cursed at him in his native language.

Not wanting to let them know that sometimes the evil threats of bad guys actually bothered him, Jack just smiled and waved them away.

Chapter 14:
The Resolution

When the commotion died down, Kate burst through the door of the airport and ran onto the runway.

'Jack!' she cried, running towards him, her arms flailing with excitement. 'You did it! You saved my mum and the treasure!' She leaped up and kissed him squarely on the lips.

Stunned, Jack stood there, not knowing what to do. The GPF could prepare you for all sorts of occasions, but not one involving a kiss from a girl. Especially a kiss from a girl you liked.

'Thank you so much for saving our lives,' said a voice from behind Kate. Jack looked past her. It was Kate's mum. 'And for saving the sacred treasure too.'

'I think you'll be needing this,' said Jack, handing the box to her. 'Hopefully it will be safer now.'

'Don't worry,' said Kate's mother. 'I'll see to it that no one finds it again.' She paused, and Jack could see that she was studying his face. 'Would you like to come back to our house and have some tea?' she asked. 'I think you probably have a few questions for me.'

Jack knew what she was talking about – his brother, Max. He had been waiting for months to find out something, anything, significant about his brother. And here was the woman who was probably the last person to see him before he disappeared. It was as if Max had sent him here to meet her.

'I'd love that,' said Jack, giving a deep, relieved sigh.

'Great!' said Kate as she grabbed Jack's hand. Reluctantly, he kept it there as she led him off the runway and they set out for her home.

Chapter 15:
The Final Clue

When they arrived back at Kate's house, they tidied up the kitchen, and Kate's mother poured them all some tea. She sat across from Jack at the kitchen table and began to tell him what she knew about Max.

'I met your brother six months ago, when I was working in Egypt,' she said. 'I was running a project, much like this one, that involved watching over something sacred. When I got word that someone was planning to steal it, I contacted the GPF and they sent Max to protect it.

'Max was fantastic,' she continued. 'He was clever and truly passionate about his job. But one day, the thing that he was guarding disappeared and so did Max. After that, I was reassigned to Cambodia. I truly don't know what happened to your brother,' she said. 'I'm sorry,' she added.

'Is there anything else you can tell me about the mission?' pleaded Jack.

'The only thing I can say is that Max's mission had something to do with a mummy.'

'A mummy?' asked Jack.

'That's all I can tell you,' said Kate's mum. 'I've already said too much.'

'Right,' said Jack, pushing back his chair and standing up. 'It looks as if I've got a bit of research to do on Egyptian mummies.' He smiled at Kate's mum. 'Thanks for telling me everything you did.'

'I hope you do find Max,' she said. 'And when you do, please tell him I said hello.'

'Will do,' said Jack. He looked at his Watch Phone. He knew what he needed to do next. He turned to Kate and her mum. 'I'd better go,' he said.

'Do you have to?' asked Kate, who was wearing a long face.

'Unfortunately I do,' he said, shrugging his shoulders. Jack was a bit sad to be leaving too. 'But you know where to reach me,' he said, 'and I know where to find you.' He smiled at the knowledge that she still had the Transponder.

Kate smiled back, happy to know that there was a chance she might see Jack again.

Jack turned to Kate's mum. 'Can I borrow your bedroom?'

She looked puzzled for a moment, but then she realized that GPF agents had to depart in secrecy. She pointed towards a door. 'Of course you can,' she said. 'It's right over there.'

Jack gave a final wave to Kate and her mum and stepped into the bedroom. He closed the door and opened the front pouch of his Secret Agent Book Bag. Inside the pocket was a small grey pellet. He pulled it out and threw it on the floor. The pellet broke open, instantly releasing a grey smoke into the air. The smoke began to drift upwards, across his body and over his eyes. Through the smoke, Jack could make out a framed photograph

of Kate and her mum.

As soon as the smoke began to move, Jack tugged on the straps of his Book Bag and yelled, 'Off to England!'

Within an instant, the smoke churned and swirled around him, sucking him into its core and transporting him back home.

When he arrived, Jack took a deep breath. He put his Book Bag under his bed and climbed into his pyjamas. As he stared up at his Magic Map, thoughts of Egypt and Max swirled around in his head.

He yawned. The time on the clock read 7:31 p.m. – it was time to get some sleep. After all, he'd had a busy evening. As he got into bed he could hear Lily's loud voice drifting up the stairs.

'And then, Mrs MacDonald made everyone stay behind after class, just because of what Simon Ryder said . . .'

Jack smiled to himself as he sank into his second deep sleep of the day.

SECRET AGENT JACK STALWART

The Search for the Sunken Treasure: AUSTRALIA

Read the first chapter here

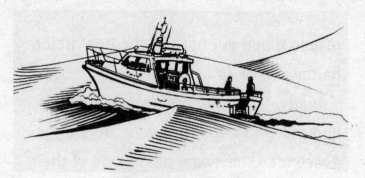

Chapter 1:
The Reef

Eighteen-year-old Alfie Doyle stood at the
back of the boat in his favourite blue
wetsuit and looked out over the rough
Australian sea. He fastened his oxygen
tank, put his mouthpiece in and took a
deep breath before jumping off.

SPLASH!

He crashed into the churning waves.
Almost instantly, he began to sink. He
checked his oxygen levels and glanced at
his watch. There was only twenty minutes
to swim to the bottom, do a bit of

research and get back to the boat before he ran out of air.

Ready, he tipped his head forward and plunged into the depths. As he descended, he swam past some of the Great Barrier Reef's amazing sea life. There were orange clown fish, purple and yellow surgeonfish, schools of blue-green puller fish and even brownish moray eels. This was the bit Alfie loved most – swimming with some of the most unusual sea creatures in the world.

Alfie continued downwards. As he approached the seabed, he flicked on his underwater torch. When his feet touched the bottom, he lifted his hand to his mouthpiece and switched on his Underwater Communications Piece.

'Touchdown,' said Alfie into the UCP. 'Will report everything as I go.' In his earpiece he could hear Harry, his boss, who was still on the boat.

'Good,' said Harry. 'Let's hope the sands haven't shifted that much.'

Alfie swam to the back of the wreck, or the stern. Last time they were there, he and Harry had discovered some pieces from the officers' quarters. From what Alfie could tell everything was as they left it forty-eight hours ago.

He carried on, swimming the length of the rotted wooden boat towards the bow at the front. The bow was where the crew members would have lived, and

Harry in particular was keen to see what was there. Today their job was to remove the sand covering the bow, bring up any relics and hand them over to the State Maritime Museum.

As Alfie raised his torch to survey the scene, he gasped. The sand that had covered the front of the wreck two days ago was no longer there. He swam a bit closer and noticed a hole going down into the area where the crew members' quarters would have been.

Alfie frantically spoke into his UCP. 'Harry, something's wrong!'

'What do you mean?' asked Harry.

'Something's not right,' said Alfie. 'There's no sand!'

As Alfie was talking, a dark figure in diving gear snuck up behind him. The stranger lifted a gun and pointed their spear directly at him.

'I think someone's taken something from HMS *Pandora*!' said Alfie, his eyes bulging with panic.

Just then, the figure pulled the trigger, releasing the deadly spear into Alfie's leg.

'Owww!' howled Alfie, blinded by the pain.

'Alfie! Alfie!' Harry called into his speaker. But there was no reply, just a crackling noise from Alfie's UCP.

SECRET-AGENT NOTES

SECRET-AGENT NOTES